Clue™

DEATH BY CANDLELIGHT

Book created by A. E. Parker

Written by Marie Jacks

Based on characters from the Parker Brothers® game

A Creative Media Applications Production

SCHOLASTIC INC.
New York Toronto London Auckland Sydney

For Zachary Harris Simko

*Special thanks to: Holly Riehl, Susan Nash,
Laura Millhollin, Maureen Taxter, Jean Feiwel,
Ellie Berger, Greg Holch, Dona Smith,
Nancy Smith, John Simko, Madalina Stefan,
David Tommasino, and Elizabeth Parisi*

ISBN 0-590-62374-5

12 11 10 9 8 7 6 5 4 3   5 6 7 8 9/9 0/0

Printed in the U.S.A.   40

First Scholastic printing, December 1995

Contents

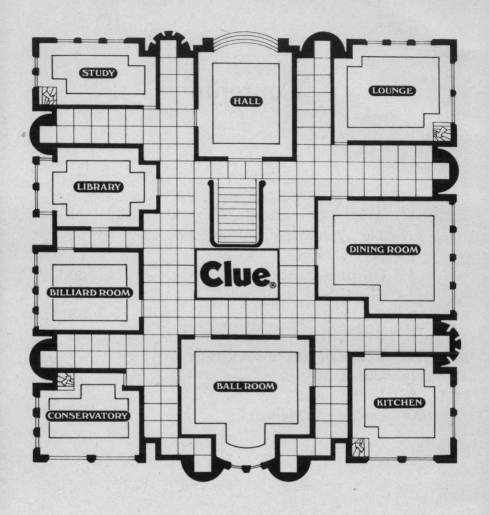

STUDY

HALL

LOUNGE

LIBRARY

Clue®

DINING ROOM

BILLIARD ROOM

BALL ROOM

KITCHEN

CONSERVATORY

Allow Me to Introduce Myself . . .

IF YOU DON'T KNOW ME BY NOW, MY name is Reginald Boddy. I am one of the world's richest men — and one of the nicest. After all, I continue to entertain a select group of guests that few other hosts would tolerate for more than a minute.

Actually, I consider these particular guests my fiends — I mean, *friends*. And I know they think I'm a good heist — I mean, *host*.

For those of you who have visited with us before, I extend a hearty "Welcome back!"

For you newcomers, well, prepare yourself for many, many surprises, including a surprise attack or two.

What's a typical weekend like here at the mansion? To give you an idea, the last visit involved screaming skeletons, robbery, murder, and very bad manners. Believe it or not, we managed to enjoy a delightful time, even if I ended up shot to death. Oh, well, one must be prepared to clean up after one's guests.

And don't worry — I learned long ago to wear

bullet-proof long johns when these particular guests come to visit.

Who are my so-called friends? In a few moments they will be joining me in the garage, where, I suspect, they will greet me with open arms. (It's when they leave with their arms wrapped around my belongings that I worry.) May I beg your assistance in helping me keep track of them?

There are six suspects — er, guests — including my loyal, if sometimes untidy maid, Mrs. White. (I will never be a suspect in any wrongdoing. You have my word on this, as a gentleman.) The six guests you need to keep track of are:

Mr. Green: He claims he's a businessman without peer. That's because he's cheated and robbed every last one of his peers. Green may be his favorite color, but gold and silver run close seconds.

Colonel Mustard: A gentleman of the old school who believes that any disagreement, no matter how minor, is best solved by a duel. Don't even think of crossing him unless you're prepared for pistols at dawn.

Mrs. Peacock: A lady who always apologizes when she sneezes — even when she's alone. Rumor has it she once sent herself to her room without supper for thinking rude thoughts.

Professor Plum: He's crammed so much learning into his mind that there's no room left for such trifling matters as where he left his keys, his wallet, his eyeglasses, or his shoes. Once he even misplaced himself.

Miss Scarlet: The woman never met a mirror she didn't like. While others reflect on life, Scarlet looks at her own reflection.

Mrs. White: As my loyal maid these many years, she knows where the bodies are buried around the mansion. If you see her approaching with a shovel, I advise you to run the other way.

There. The best of friends, I can assure you.

Please know that at the end of each chapter a list of suspects, weapons, and rooms will be provided so that you can keep track of the goings-on at the mansion during your visit. I hope you're rested, well-fed, and ready, because it's time to dive into our first caper and curse — I mean, *chapter* and *verse*. I'll see you at the end of the book — if we both come through this alive. Cheers!

1.
The White Elephant Murder

ON FRIDAY AFTERNOON, MR. BODDY'S usual guests — Mr. Green, Colonel Mustard, Mrs. Peacock, Professor Plum, and Miss Scarlet — arrived at his mansion for the weekend. But no one answered the front door.

"That's funny," said Colonel Mustard.

"I don't find it funny at all!" fumed Mrs. Peacock. "It's very rude to keep one's guests waiting in the cold!"

"I wonder where Mrs. White is?" asked Mr. Green. "She's Mr. Boddy's maid. It's her job to answer the doorbell."

"Perhaps *this* is our answer," suggested Miss Scarlet, pointing a long, polished, red fingernail at a note taped to the front door.

My dear friends,
Please proceed directly to the garage at the side of the mansion.

Your host,
Reginald Boddy

4

"I hope Mr. Boddy doesn't expect us to work on one of his many cars," said Professor Plum. "I don't know the difference between a spark plug and a fan belt."

"Why am I not surprised?" replied Miss Scarlet snootily. "Well, I'm not dirtying my hands, that's for certain."

"Neither am I," agreed Mr. Green. "Unless there's a good sum of money involved."

"Asking us to join him in the garage, of all places," added Mrs. Peacock. "What a particularly bad show of manners!"

"Now, let's not prejudge our host," cautioned Colonel Mustard. "I'm sure Boddy has the best of motives. However, if he doesn't, I'll challenge the scoundrel to a duel!"

Grumbling and complaining, the guests walked around to the side of the mansion, where they could see the doors to Mr. Boddy's twelve-car garage wide open.

Inside, they found Mr. Boddy and Mrs. White sorting through an enormous pile of boxes.

"How very, very rude!" snapped Mrs. Peacock. "You invite us for the weekend, but no one answers the front door. Then you ask us to come out here to this musty, dusty garage! This is absolute rubbish!"

"Good, you're all here. Welcome to what I hope shall be another lively visit." Mr. Boddy straight-

5

ened and dusted off his clothing. He gestured to the boxes and added, "Indeed it is rubbish, as you can see. And I do apologize, Mrs. Peacock. I'm afraid I got carried away."

"And if you're not careful," said Mrs. White, "you might all get carried away, too — carried away with the rest of this junk tomorrow."

"What do you mean by that?" demanded Mr. Green.

"Actually," Mr. Boddy explained, "it's high time I rid myself of things I no longer need. So I'm having a white elephant sale tomorrow morning and donating all the proceeds to charity."

Professor Plum scratched his head. "Did I hear you correctly? You're selling Mrs. White and elephants tomorrow?"

"A white elephant sale means a junk sale," replied Mr. Boddy. "To sell things a person doesn't want anymore."

"Well, that explains why you're selling Mrs. White," said Professor Plum with a smirk.

Mrs. White gave Professor Plum a fiery look and continued her work.

Mr. Boddy opened a box and uncovered an old ice bucket. "My gosh," he exclaimed. "Another ice bucket!"

Miss Scarlet stepped forward to examine it. "Is it silver?" she asked hopefully.

"Gold plated?" asked Mr. Green.

"A valuable antique?" asked Mrs. Peacock.

6

"Tin," Mr. Boddy said, "and rather new, I'm afraid."

"Drat!" said Colonel Mustard.

"Why bother to keep it?" said Professor Plum.

"Junk it," Miss Scarlet replied.

Mr. Boddy added the ice bucket to a growing heap of items to be sold.

"I'm all for getting rid of unnecessary objects. That's how I explain most of my duels," said Colonel Mustard. "But why did you invite us this weekend, since you already had plans?"

"I thought," said Mr. Boddy, "that you might want to help me."

The guests laughed and laughed until Mr. Boddy stopped them with a stare.

"Come on," he said. "Who's going to step forward first and offer me a hand?"

"Busy, must be going," said Colonel Mustard.

"Sorry, can't stay," said Mr. Green.

"Just remembered some other plans," said Professor Plum.

"Please forgive me, but no," said Mrs. Peacock.

"Forgot to feed my cat," purred Scarlet, heading for the door.

"Wait!" said Mr. Boddy. "If you help me, you may each pick something from the white elephant sale to keep for your very own. There are treasures mixed in with the junk."

7

"Treasures?" asked Mrs. Peacock, looking at the scattered boxes with doubt.

"I hope you don't mean that tin ice bucket!" sneered Mr. Green.

"Treasures," Mr. Boddy insisted. "Old jewelry. Rare books. Antique figurines. All sorts of valuable things."

"Treasures," echoed Miss Scarlet. "In that case, my cat can wait to be fed."

"Where should I start?" asked Professor Plum. "At the beginning?"

"Here, let me help," said Colonel Mustard, taking a box from Mrs. White.

Mr. Green dove into another box. "Anything to be of service," he said, ripping the wrapping paper to shreds.

"There's even a valuable old marble elephant somewhere in here," said Mr. Boddy. "My grandfather brought it back from India. It's only worth several thousand dollars because its trunk is chipped."

"An elephant?" said Professor Plum. "It must be huge!"

"Oh, it isn't life-size," chuckled Mr. Boddy. "It's a miniature elephant that fits in the palm of your hand."

"A miniature elephant," replied Mr. Green. "That makes as much sense as saying jumbo shrimp!"

"It's small, but made of solid marble," said Mr. Boddy. "And its eyes are rubies and its toenails are solid gold."

"If it's so valuable, why get rid of it?" asked Miss Scarlet.

"Because I have several others just like it," said Mr. Boddy. "And because its sale will benefit charity."

"It *is* the right thing to do," said Mrs. Peacock with a nod. She opened yet another box and inspected its contents. "Just as it's polite to help a friend."

"Yes, yes," Professor Plum added. "Let's make this the biggest miniature elephant — I mean, *white* elephant — sale ever!"

"Wait until I get my hands on that marble elephant," Mrs. White whispered to Colonel Mustard.

"I'll beat you to it!" said Colonel Mustard. "After all, it's worth several thousand dollars."

"I'll find it first," boasted Mr. Green.

"No, *I* will!" exclaimed Miss Scarlet.

"The elephant is mine," predicted Mrs. Peacock.

But an hour later, the elephant had not yet been found.

"Well, it's getting late," Mr. Boddy said, "so let's call it a day. We can finish this right after breakfast tomorrow. Let's all meet back here in the garage at nine o'clock sharp to set up for the sale."

"What about the elephant?" asked Professor Plum.

"The elephant has been in one of these boxes for years," said Mr. Boddy. "Another night won't make any difference." He shook the hand of each of his guests and said, "Thank you for helping."

Then Mr. Boddy turned to Mrs. White and said, "Please take my good friends inside for a spot of tea."

"Trash!" muttered Mrs. White, looking at the guests.

"I beg your pardon?" demanded Mrs. Peacock.

"I said there's a lot of trash to be collected before the morning." With a gleam in her eye, Mrs. White then led the guests inside for tea.

Later that night . . .

Later that night, when the guests were supposed to be sleeping, someone slipped out of the mansion and sneaked off to the garage.

"It has to be here somewhere," he whispered, rustling around in the pile of boxes. "Ah!" he exclaimed several minutes later when he found something smooth and heavy. It was the marble elephant!

Making sure no one was watching, he tucked the elephant inside his blue bathrobe. "An elephant never forgets, and I'll never forget this elephant," he told himself. "And how easy it was to steal it!"

He carefully carried his treasure back into the mansion.

But just as he closed the door to the Hall, he was hit over the head with the Lead Pipe. Wounded, he sank to the floor. His bathrobe fell open and the marble elephant fell free.

The attacker dropped the weapon and took the treasure to the Library.

Hearing some noise, another guest entered the Hall to find out what had happened. She saw the fallen guest and shook her head. "Trash, all of them. Sneaking around at night! Stealing Mr. Boddy's treasure!" She took a weapon from her pocket and left.

The guest in the Library was moving some books, planning to hide the elephant behind them, when she was surprised by a guest with the Knife. "Hand over that elephant, madam. I'd hate to challenge you to a duel."

"Elephant? What elephant?"

"I'm not referring to Dumbo! Hand it over!" the guest with the Knife ordered.

The woman handed the elephant to him. He ran with his treasure toward the Study.

But on the way, he ran right into Miss Scarlet,

who had just fled the Hall, where she had seen a dead body.

Both Miss Scarlet and the man screamed in surprise.

The elephant went flying. Luckily, it landed on the rug and was not damaged.

"What's going on?" the man asked Miss Scarlet. "Why are you screaming?"

"There's a dead body in the Hall!" replied Miss Scarlet. "Lying there in a blue bathrobe."

"How strange," said the man. "Who is it?"

"I didn't stop to check!" snapped Miss Scarlet. "All I saw was a blue bathrobe and a pair of hairy legs!" Suddenly, she saw the marble elephant on the floor. Before the man could react, she grabbed it.

"Give that back to me!" shouted the man. "It's mine!"

"Not anymore!" said Miss Scarlet as she ran back to the Hall. "I'm packing this pachyderm in my very own trunk and leaving this circus!"

In the Hall, Miss Scarlet found a very confused Professor Plum standing barefoot in his red bathrobe.

"Good evening. Strange time for you to be jogging," he said, as she sped by.

"Strange time for you to be awake," she retorted.

"I thought I heard some screaming," he said.

Miss Scarlet stopped suddenly, and looked around. Then she screamed. "It's gone!" she shouted. "The body is gone!"

"Mr. Boddy?" Professor Plum asked. "I'm sure he's upstairs, asleep!"

"Not *Mr.* Boddy, you fool!" said Miss Scarlet. "*The* body!"

Professor Plum scratched his head again.

The guest who first used the Lead Pipe joined the hubbub in the Hall.

She saw Miss Scarlet with the elephant. "I had it first!" she cried. "Give it back to me!"

"You're as slow as an elephant if you think I'm handing this over to you, Mrs. Peacock!" mocked Miss Scarlet.

To everyone's surprise, a voice boomed from the Hall closet, "Don't anyone move! Give me the elephant or I'll shoot!" An arm in a blue bathrobe emerged from inside the closet, holding a dangerous weapon.

"That's the dead body," said a shocked Miss Scarlet. "It was wearing the blue robe!" Very frightened, she handed over the elephant.

But just then, the closet door burst completely open, revealing two people inside. One was wearing a blue bathrobe and another had hairy legs and was wearing an old-fashioned nightshirt. A male voice said from the closet, "First my elephant is taken from me and now my robe!"

13

WHO WAS THE FIRST THIEF IN THE BLUE BATHROBE?

WHO IS THE LAST THIEF IN THE BLUE BATHROBE?

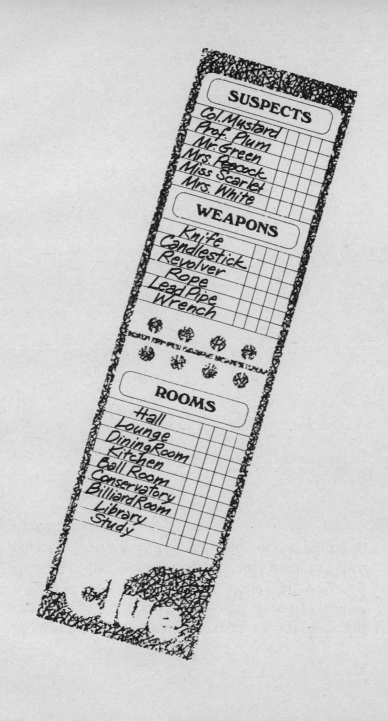

blow and Mr. Boddy awoke from a deep sleep and came to see what had happened. After Mrs. White returned the elephant to Mr. Boddy, they agreed that all of her week's wages would be donated to charity, along with the proceeds of the white elephant sale.

SOLUTION

MR. GREEN was the first thief.

MRS. WHITE in the HALL with the REVOLVER is the second thief.

The male guest originally wearing the blue robe was attacked in the Hall with the Lead Pipe. The attacker fled with the elephant to the Library and was confronted by Colonel Mustard. We know it is Colonel Mustard because he challenged the guest to a duel, and we learn that the guest is female because Colonel Mustard called her "madam."

Later, Colonel Mustard was tripped by Miss Scarlet, whose screams brought Professor Plum downstairs. Since we can now account for Colonel Mustard and Professor Plum, we know that Mr. Green was the thief in the blue bathrobe. They were joined in the Hall by the original female attacker, who was identified as Mrs. Peacock by Miss Scarlet. Since we can eliminate Peacock, Mustard, Scarlet, and Plum, the two suspects are Mr. Green and Mrs. White. Mrs. White obviously put on Mr. Green's robe and put Mr. Green in the closet, where his hairy legs led to his identification. We know Mrs. White had the Revolver because she threatened to shoot.

Fortunately, Mr. Green recovered from his

2.
Boddy's Byte

Mr. BODDY CALLED HIS GUESTS TOgether in the Library. After tea and snacks were served, he cleared his throat and got down to business.

"Ladies and gentlemen, please don't take offense," he began. "But after your last visit I took an inventory of the mansion and sadly discovered many of my beloved possessions were missing."

"Well, maybe you simply forgot where you left them," suggested Professor Plum. "That's what happens to me."

"Or maybe you looked in the wrong places," suggested Miss Scarlet.

"Or maybe Mrs. White hid them," suggested Mr. Green.

"Or maybe *you* stole them!" Mrs. White shot back.

"Frankly, I don't care what happened," Mr. Boddy said. "The point is, I've decided I can no longer tolerate things disappearing right from under my nose."

"Has someone stolen Boddy's mustache?" asked a bewildered Professor Plum.

"You know," Colonel Mustard told Mr. Boddy, "if you gave us all your things, you wouldn't have to worry about them."

"Now there's a novel solution," said Miss Scarlet, taking a book down from a shelf.

"I came up with a better solution," Mr. Boddy said. "I've installed a new and improved computerized security system in the mansion."

"That's no solution — that's an insult!" stormed Colonel Mustard. "Mr. Boddy, I'd challenge you to a duel — if I didn't think it improper to kill our host. What do you take us for?"

"Sneaks and thieves, for starters," replied Mr. Boddy.

"Talk about bad manners!" snorted Mrs. Peacock. "How dare you call us by those awful names!"

"Yes," agreed Professor Plum. "I have half a mind to leave the mansion right now!"

"Once he locates the other half," sneered Mrs. White.

"The nerve! Why, I've never stolen a thing in my entire life," protested Miss Scarlet, slipping a sterling silver teaspoon into her purse.

"Good gosh, Boddy," added Mr. Green. "If you don't want your things stolen, then you shouldn't leave them lying around like you do."

"Lying around?" Mr. Boddy echoed.

"Yes," Mr. Green nodded. "You have your paintings hanging right on the walls. You leave your rare books out in the open here in the Library. Silverware stashed away in a Kitchen drawer for anyone to get at. Pardon me, sir, but you've only yourself to blame when something disappears."

"Please understand," pleaded Mr. Boddy. "My aim is not to offend — but I must protect my valuables."

"But if you guard everything under lock and key, what are we going to do all weekend long?" asked Miss Scarlet. "We'll die of boredom!"

"Please, " continued Mr. Boddy. "The new and improved computerized system will not interfere with your stay."

"We'll be the judge of that!" insisted Mrs. Peacock. "What exactly is this new and improved system?"

"Every room in the mansion has been electronically hooked up to a computer," explained Mr. Boddy. "To enter a room, a guest must type in his or her secret password. When the computer recognizes the proper password, the door is released."

"So it's like being buzzed into a friend's apartment building?" asked Colonel Mustard.

"Precisely," Mr. Boddy said with a nod.

"I don't like it," said Mrs. Peacock, "but I suppose it seems polite enough."

"One last thing," added Mr. Boddy. "The computer keeps a record of which guests enter which rooms — so I always know who is where."

"So your byte *is* worse than your bark!" joked Miss Scarlet.

"But will it work?" asked Mr. Green. "I'm not about to waste my time with passwords if the system is full of bugs."

"Bugs?" repeated Professor Plum. "Is Boddy having army ants guarding his things?"

"There are no bugs. The system has been thoroughly tested," Mr. Boddy assured his guests. "Now I need to assign each of you your own secret password. Colonel, you're first."

Mr. Boddy motioned Colonel Mustard over to the corner, where they could talk privately.

"Colonel," Mr. Boddy whispered, "your secret password is DUEL."

"I'll have no trouble remembering that," Colonel Mustard said.

Once Colonel Mustard returned to his seat, Mr. Boddy asked Mrs. Peacock to come forward.

"Mrs. Peacock," he told her, "your secret password is MANNERS."

She approved.

Professor Plum was next.

"Professor, your secret password is PUDDING."

"Pudding?" Professor Plum repeated a little too loudly, allowing Colonel Mustard to overhear. "Why pudding?"

"Plum pudding," Mr. Boddy explained.

"Oh, of course," said the professor, who happily returned to his seat.

Mr. Green followed.

"Mr. Green, I thought the password WEALTH would fit you," said Mr. Boddy.

"To a tee," Mr. Green said, pleased. He liked the password so much he wrote it down in his little black appointment book.

Miss Scarlet was next.

Mr. Boddy asked, "Miss Scarlet, would you like the password RUBY?"

"I'd rather have the real thing," she said, "but, yes, that will do."

Returning to her seat, Miss Scarlet whispered to Colonel Mustard, "I'll tell you my password if you tell me yours."

Flattered, Colonel Mustard agreed and whispered his secret password back to Miss Scarlet. But when it was her turn, Miss Scarlet said her password was JADE.

The last person to receive a secret password was Mrs. White.

"How about APRON?" suggested Mr. Boddy. "Since you always wear one?"

"I have to, with all the work I do," Mrs. White grumbled.

Returning to the other guests, Mrs. White "accidentally" bumped into Mr. Green and pickpocketed his appointment book.

"Thank you for your cooperation," Mr. Boddy told them all. "Now, if you will excuse me, I need to go to the Conservatory to examine the latest priceless addition to my coin collection."

"What is it?" asked Mrs. White.

"I'd rather not say," said Mr. Boddy.

"Well, if your new and improved computerized security system is any good, why keep it a secret?" asked a clever Miss Scarlet.

Mr. Boddy thought for a moment, then said, "You're absolutely right. There's no way anyone can steal anything without my knowing it. My latest addition is a solid-gold coin retrieved from the wreck of a seventeenth-century Spanish ship."

The guests looked at one another. Secretly, each one was already plotting how to get the best of Mr. Boddy's new and improved computerized security system and steal the valuable coin.

Several hours later . . .

Several hours later, as Mr. Boddy was examining the coin in the Conservatory, a guest typed the password WEALTH into the computer and entered the Lounge. The guest took the Revolver, which had been hidden there.

Outside the Kitchen, another guest typed the

23

password PUDDING into the computer. The Kitchen door released, and the guest entered. To his delight, the guest found some plum pudding in the refrigerator, which he greedily devoured. Then he removed a Knife from the drawer and quickly exited.

At the same time, Colonel Mustard, in the Billiard Room, freed the Lead Pipe he had previously taped under the billiard table. "We'll see how Boddy's computerized system stands up to this," he said, waving the weapon.

Upstairs, a female guest who knew no other password but her own went to bed and soon fell asleep.

Downstairs, still another guest typed the password APRON into the computer outside the Study, and gained entry. There she took the Candlestick off the mantel.

Meanwhile, another guest finished a snack of caviar in the Dining Room and opened her purse. Smiling, she saw a weapon inside.

A minute later . . .

A minute later, a guest typed the password JADE into the computer outside the Conservatory door.

But since JADE was not a correct password, he could not gain access.

"Why, that double-crossing — !" But before he

could finish, he was hit over the head with the Candlestick and fell to the floor.

The person with the Candlestick typed the password WEALTH into the computer.

The computer recognized a correct password and released the door.

The person entered the Conservatory. Then the person sneaked up on Mr. Boddy, knocked him out, and stole the gold coin.

"Your new and improved computerized security system can't hold a candle to my cleverness!" the thief mocked.

The thief ran down the Hall — and was immediately attacked by the guest holding the Knife. "Allow me to cut in," the guest taunted.

The guest with the Knife grabbed the coin and gained access to the Hall by typing the password PUDDING in the computer outside the door.

But once inside the Hall, he accidentally knocked down one of Mr. Boddy's prized suits of armor. It toppled over the guest, making a loud clanking noise.

Hearing the commotion, a different guest typed the password WEALTH into the computer outside the Hall and quickly entered.

"It looks like a bad *knight* for you," the male guest told the guest lying on the floor. He wrestled the coin away and fled.

The guest now holding the coin rushed to the computer table located just outside the Dining

Room door. There he typed his password on the keyboard and gained entry.

Inside the Dining Room, he was about to hide the coin under a stack of Boddy's best china plates when he was attacked with the Candlestick and knocked out.

The guest took the coin, went through the victim's pockets, left the Dining Room, raced across the mansion, and typed the password WEALTH into the computer outside of the Lounge.

The guest was about to enter, but was attacked from behind with a blunt instrument that was *not* the Lead Pipe.

The attacker grabbed the coin — and a black appointment book found in the victim's pocket — and went to the room on the other side of the Hall. There this guest typed the password WEALTH into the computer, and entered.

"*Wealth* is definitely the right password," the guest joked, eyeing the prized gold coin. The guest hid the coin in the room, and then went to bed as if nothing had happened.

WHICH THIEF HID THE COIN . . . AND WHERE?

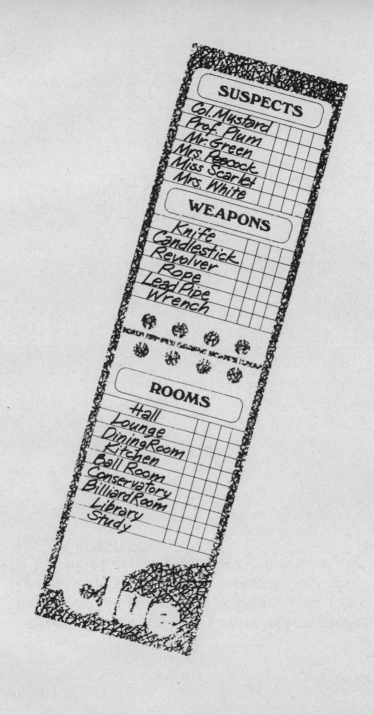

Unfortunately, Mr. Boddy never told his guests that the computer was also recording their comings and goings on video. Now caught, Miss Scarlet had to return the coin, and her password was changed to THIEF.

SOLUTION

MISS SCARLET in the STUDY

It's important to know which guests know passwords other than their own. We know that Colonel Mustard overheard Professor Plum, that Miss Scarlet tricked Colonel Mustard into telling his, and that Mrs. White pickpocketed Mr. Green's black appointment book, which contained his password.

Later, Mrs. White attacked Colonel Mustard after he entered Miss Scarlet's false password. Mrs. White attacked Mr. Boddy and stole the coin; but in turn was attacked by Professor Plum. Although both Mrs. White and Mr. Green knew the password WEALTH, it was a male guest who wrestled the coin from Professor Plum, so it must have been Mr. Green. Mr. Green moved to the Dining Room and was attacked by Mrs. White with the Candlestick. Mrs. White, in turn, was attacked by Miss Scarlet, who had the blunt instrument that was *not* the Lead Pipe. Miss Scarlet stole not only the coin, but Mr. Green's appointment book. Thus, it was Miss Scarlet who used Mr. Green's password to gain access to the Study, which is the room on the other side of the Hall from the Lounge.

3.
Creature Features

IT HAD BEEN SNOWING FOR HOURS AND there was no sign of the storm letting up.

"If this snow doesn't stop soon, we may be stuck here at the mansion for a week," predicted Professor Plum.

Mrs. White shuddered. "Perish the thought," she said.

"This snow makes for very cold and slippery dueling," complained Colonel Mustard.

"I say we make the most of it," suggested Mrs. Peacock. "This is the perfect opportunity for me to present another in my on-going series of lectures on good manners."

"In that case, this is the perfect opportunity for us to make a quick exit," Mr. Green whispered to Miss Scarlet.

"I agree," whispered Miss Scarlet. "I'd rather stand in the snow than sit through another one of Mrs. Peacock's lectures."

But no one was more disappointed than Mr. Boddy. The snow had forced him to cancel his annual badminton contest.

"I'm so sorry," he told his guests. "I know you were looking forward to some competitive badminton as much as I."

Professor Plum continued to stand by the window, staring out at the storm. "I haven't seen snow like this since the last blizzard," he informed the group. "Whenever that was."

"I'm afraid no one's going out in this weather," insisted Mr. Boddy. "It's not fit for man or beast — or woman, for that matter."

"Rats!" moaned Colonel Mustard. "I was ready to wager a thousand dollars that I'd beat Mr. Green at badminton this year."

"A thousand dollars?" said Mr. Green. "I'll play you in this freezing mess for that sort of money!"

"I'm disappointed, too," said Miss Scarlet. "After all, there's nothing quite as exciting as badminton. Unless it's sleeping," she added sarcastically.

"Well, since none of you wish to learn good manners," said Mrs. Peacock, "I'm going to wrap myself up in a blanket, sit by the fire, and read the latest book on etiquette."

"And I might as well go to the Dining Room and steal — I mean, *polish* the silver," said Mrs. White with a sigh.

"I'll just stand here by the window, watching the snow, lost in my thoughts," announced Professor Plum.

"It's easy to understand why you'd be lost in your thoughts," joked Colonel Mustard.

"Actually, I have a better idea," announced Mr. Boddy. "When I heard that the weather might take a turn for the worse, I rented some of my favorite movies on video."

"Your favorite movies?" asked Mrs. White. "Probably with cute cartoon animals who sing silly songs in squeaky voices."

"You're way off," replied Mr. Boddy, smiling.

"I imagine you relish a good war movie — like I do," guessed Colonel Mustard. "Nothing like a good battle to cheer a man up. Right, Boddy?"

"Wrong," answered Mr. Boddy, still smiling.

"Our host is a secret romantic," observed Miss Scarlet. "I bet he rented a stack of Hollywood's greatest love stories. That's why you're holding a box of tissues, am I right? To wipe the tears from your eyes when the lovers must part?"

Mr. Boddy grinned and shook his head. "Wrong again. Actually, this snow has given me a bit of a cold," he said, wiping his nose with a tissue. "Miss Scarlet, I'll leave the love stories to you."

"Well, I'm certain that a gentleman of Mr. Boddy's refinement selected costume dramas," said Mrs. Peacock. "Movies set in times gone by, where people's dress and behavior were proper, no matter what the situation."

"Pardon me," said Mr. Boddy, "but you're incorrect, too."

"I know Boddy like the back of my hand," said Mr. Green. "His kind of movie is my kind of movie. Rags-to-riches stories of characters who accumulate great fortunes."

"Nope," replied Mr. Boddy.

The group turned to Professor Plum. "Professor," asked Mustard, "what type of movie do you think our host prefers?"

Professor Plum thought for a moment, and then snapped his fingers. "I know! Musicals with plenty of catchy feet and dancing songs. I mean, catchy songs and dancing feet." Professor Plum began to tap-dance across the floor. Sadly, though, he tripped over his own feet and fell down.

"The truth is, I love scary monster movies," Mr. Boddy said, helping Professor Plum to his feet. "You know, creature features."

"Creature features?" repeated Mr. Green. "You mean like Mustard's home movies of Thanksgiving with his relatives."

"Take that back," snarled Colonel Mustard, "or I'll challenge you to a duel."

"Calm down!" Mr. Boddy said hastily. "I mean classics like *Frankenstein*, *Dracula*, *The Mummy*, *The Creature From the Black Lagoon*, and *Godzilla*," said Mr. Boddy. "Flicks that raise goose bumps on the arms."

"I've often wondered what happens to geese when they're afraid," mused Professor Plum. "Do they get people bumps on their wings?"

"I think monsters are rude!" exclaimed Mrs. Peacock. "Name one monster who ever displayed good manners."

"Count Dracula always said 'Good evening' when he entered a room," replied Mr. Boddy.

Mrs. Peacock reluctantly conceded the point.

"A bone-chilling video might warm us up on such a cold day," suggested Miss Scarlet.

"That's the spirit," nodded Mr. Boddy. "Let's watch them together in the Lounge. Mrs. White, would you be so kind as to make us a gigantic bowl of popcorn?"

"Make mine hot-air style with no toppings," said Colonel Mustard, "because I need to remain in tip-top condition for dueling."

"Plain kernels for the Colonel," noted Mrs. White.

"Personally, I like popcorn with butter," Professor Plum said. "But no salt. Too much salt is very bad for the heart, you know."

"Make mine with salt *and* butter," Miss Scarlet requested. "What good is life — and popcorn — if you don't enjoy it?"

"Very well, I'll join in," said Mrs. Peacock. "But the first time a monster kills someone with its bare hands, I'm leaving. As far as popcorn, I want margarine, but no salt. That's the sensible way to go."

"Salt only," Mr. Green said. "I dislike margarine and butter. They make my fingers greasy. Which can be a problem when you spend your days counting money, as I do."

"Fine," sneered Mrs. White, rolling her eyes. "I'll make five different bowls."

"What about you?" Mr. Boddy asked her. "What's your preference?"

Looking at the other guests, Mrs. White faked a smile and said, "For some reason I've lost my appetite."

Several hours later . . .

Several hours later, the guests were finishing their third creature feature.

"I haven't been this scared since I spoke with my tax attorney," said Mr. Green, wiping sweat from his brow.

Miss Scarlet added, "I haven't been this frightened since the store rejected my credit card."

"I can't remember the last time I had such a shock," Professor Plum said. "Then again, I can't remember the last time I didn't."

"The proper thing to do is to close your eyes during the scary parts," observed Mrs. Peacock.

It was nearly midnight, and Mrs. White was exhausted.

"How can you be tired?" Miss Scarlet asked.

Mrs. White nearly fainted. "Oh, perhaps it has something to do with making breakfast, lunch, and dinner for you all," she complained. "And making six beds, cleaning six rooms, and doing six loads of laundry while every one of you rings me to hurry and bring various snacks and drinks to every room in the mansion. Good night!"

"I was just asking," Miss Scarlet said with a shrug.

"Maybe if you hadn't compared Mrs. White to the Bride of Frankenstein, she might have stayed," suggested Mr. Green.

"I meant it as a compliment," Miss Scarlet said in her own defense.

"Quiet!" boomed Colonel Mustard. "Or you'll miss the part where Godzilla destroys the entire city of Tokyo. And people complain about *my* temper."

Halfway into the next movie, Mr. Boddy yawned. "Excuse me," he apologized. "But I'm ready for bed myself."

"But this was your idea," Mrs. Peacock reminded him.

"Please, stay as long as you wish," Mr. Boddy said. Standing up, he didn't notice when his gold pocket watch dropped into the bowl of popcorn topped only with salt.

But, everyone — except Mr. Boddy and the

guest into whose bowl the watch dropped — took note.

"Well, good night, dear guests," Mr. Boddy said and exited.

"I, for one, plan on watching movies all night," Professor Plum said. "After watching these creature features, I'd never get to sleep, anyway. Or if I did, I'd have terrible nightmares. It's impossible for me to sleep when I'm having nightmares. . . ."

Ignoring Professor Plum's rambling, the guest whose popcorn had no toppings reached for the bowl topped only with salt. "Allow me to take this back to the Kitchen and refill it for you."

"That's most kind, but I'm not finished." The second guest reached into the bowl and felt the pocket watch. Creating a diversion, he pointed with his other hand to the TV. "Look! Here comes the scary part!"

When the other guests looked, the man quickly transferred the watch to the bowl topped with butter and salt.

"That part wasn't so scary," Colonel Mustard said, waving a hand at the TV. "I've seen scarier things on the comics page." He stood and told the others, "Don't bother pausing the video. I'm off to the Kitchen."

"In that case," Mr. Green said, "would you be so kind as to take my bowl with you? I'd like some more, after all."

"My pleasure," said a grinning Colonel Mustard.

"I could use a bit more myself," Miss Scarlet said. Without taking her eyes off the TV, she held up her half-empty bowl.

"But I have only two hands," Colonel Mustard told her.

"Here," Mrs. Peacock volunteered. "I'll help."

"Allow me!" said Mr. Green.

"How proper of you to offer, sir, but it's taken care of," Mrs. Peacock said. She picked up her bowl and Miss Scarlet's and followed Colonel Mustard toward the Kitchen.

Left behind, Mr. Green wrestled Professor Plum for Plum's bowl. "What's got into you, Green?" the professor asked.

"I'm trying to get you some more popcorn, you dunce," Mr. Green shot back, yanking at the bowl.

"But I'm not done," the professor protested.

"You are now!" announced Mr. Green, who finally succeeded in grabbing the bowl.

Green took off after Colonel Mustard and Mrs. Peacock.

"Something's afoot," Miss Scarlet said. Not to be left out, she pursued the others.

In the Hall, Mrs. Peacock lagged behind Colonel Mustard so she could try some of Miss Scarlet's tempting popcorn. She devoured a handful and then licked her fingers. "I hope no one saw that," she said to herself. "If they did, I'll be drummed out of the Etiquette Society."

She glanced down at the popcorn coated in a luscious topping. "Oh, another handful won't kill me." Reaching into the bowl, she felt something unexpected. "This is a treat!" she told herself. "I'll just put this in my bowl for safekeeping."

Ahead, Colonel Mustard was the first to reach the Kitchen. he quickly dumped the contents of Mr. Green's bowl into the sink. To his horror, the watch was missing.

Mrs. Peacock entered and put her bowl down closest to the sink. She left Miss Scarlet's bowl next to the popcorn maker. "Is there a problem, Colonel?" she asked.

"I think that unpleasant fellow, Mr. Green, has double-crossed me," Colonel Mustard said.

Mr. Green entered and put Professor Plum's bowl down next to Mrs. Peacock's. "Did I just hear my name?"

"Green, you snake!" Colonel Mustard stormed. "Prepare to defend yourself!"

"Later," Mr. Green said. "I don't want to miss any of the movie." Quickly he snatched Miss Scarlet's bowl and left.

Colonel Mustard was about to go after him when Miss Scarlet entered and blocked his path. "Colonel, what's the hurry?" she asked.

"That scoundrel Green thinks he's gotten the best of me," Colonel Mustard replied.

"The best of you can't be worth very much," Miss Scarlet said and seized Mrs. Peacock's bowl, mistaking it for her own. She followed Mr. Green back to the Lounge.

"You promised to refill these bowls," Mrs. Peacock reminded Colonel Mustard. "If you're a gentleman, you'll forget your feud with Mr. Green and keep your promise."

So Colonel Mustard and Mrs. Peacock refilled the remaining bowls and then returned to the Lounge.

Resuming their seats in front of the TV, Mr. Green reached into Miss Scarlet's popcorn but didn't find the watch buried at the bottom.

When Colonel Mustard arrived, he said, "Mr. Green, I believe you took the wrong bowl."

"Did I?" Mr. Green asked innocently.

"Yes. You took Miss Scarlet's by mistake," Colonel Mustard said.

"Perhaps you're right," Mr. Green replied.

"Where's my popcorn?" asked Professor Plum.

"Here," Mrs. Peacock said, handing him a bowl.

"Miss Scarlet," asked Mr. Green, "care to have your own bowl back?"

"If it'll keep you quiet through the rest of the movie, fine," Miss Scarlet said, trading bowls with Mr. Green.

"Did I miss the scary part?" asked Mrs. Peacock, resuming her seat.

Colonel Mustard reached into his bowl for a handful of popcorn and said, "Watch!"

WHO HAS BODDY'S GOLD POCKET WATCH?

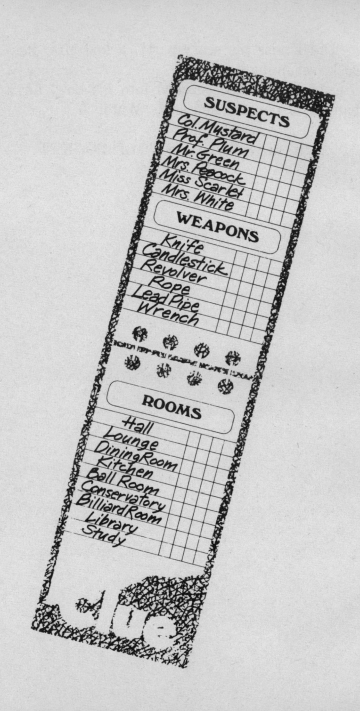

SOLUTION

MR. GREEN

We can eliminate Mrs. White because she wasn't interested in popcorn or the movies. When Mr. Boddy stood, he accidentally dropped his watch into Mr. Green's salty popcorn. Mr. Green then secretly transferred the watch into Miss Scarlet's buttery and salty bowl, which Mrs. Peacock discovered on the way to the Kitchen. Then Miss Scarlet picked up Mrs. Peacock's bowl by mistake.

Back in the Lounge, when Miss Scarlet exchanged bowls with Mr. Green, she had no idea she was giving him Mr. Boddy's watch. The problem was, neither did Mr. Green. So, absorbed in the movie, he didn't notice when he bit into Mr. Boddy's watch. As a result, he had to buy Boddy a new watch and himself a bridge of false teeth.

4.
The Fake Fruit Frolic

EARLY ONE AFTERNOON, AFTER EN-
joying a fine lunch in the Dining Room, the guests
moved to the Lounge to wait for dessert.

"I hope Mrs. White serves her famous baked
Alaska," said Miss Scarlet.

"Baked *Alaska?*" repeated Professor Plum. "It
sounds enormous! Personally, I much prefer Mrs.
White's apple pie," he added. "Delicious. Just like
my dear old Granny Smith used to make."

"Fruit and cheese is the only proper dessert,"
announced Mrs. Peacock.

"Well, you can nibble on that stuff like a well-
behaved bunny," Mr. Green said. "But ask me,
and I'll tell you there's nothing like a hot fudge
sundae with lots of whipped cream, nuts, and a
cherry on top to complete a splendid meal."

"A slice of poppy seed cake would hit the spot,"
said Colonel Mustard.

A moment later, Mrs. White entered carrying
a silver bowl loaded to the brim with beautiful,
shiny fruit.

Mrs. Peacock nodded in approval.

"Cantaloupe!" exclaimed Mr. Green.

"You're darn right I *can't elope*," said Mrs. White.

Miss Scarlet eyed the selection. "Ah, passion fruit," she said. "As you can imagine, it's my favorite."

"Mrs. White, be a *peach* and let me eat one," said Mr. Green.

"Yes, yes," agreed Colonel Mustard. "Give me a *pair* of pears."

"Don't touch that fruit!" screamed Mrs. White, just as Mrs. Peacock reached for a shiny, ripe apple.

"Good heavens!" said a startled Mrs. Peacock. "You scared me! How rude! I simply wanted a piece of fresh fruit. It's a very healthy snack, you know."

"Not this fruit," replied Mrs. White, grabbing the silver bowl from the table in the Lounge and clutching it in her arms.

"How selfish of you, taking the fruit all for yourself," complained Colonel Mustard. "I think you need to *melon* out — I mean, mellow out!"

"I don't give a fig what you think!" retorted Mrs. White.

"The fruit looks fine to me," said Professor Plum. "Is there any *raisin* why I can't have a few grapes?"

"I'll give you a *raisin* — I mean, a reason," snarled Mrs. White. "This fruit is fake."

"Did I hear you mention fruitcake?" asked Mr. Green. "Granted, fruitcake is not a hot fudge sundae, but I'll try some."

"Fake fruit!" said Mrs. White. "I've been trying to tell all of you that this fruit isn't edible."

"You mean those are poison berries?" asked Professor Plum.

"No, they're boysenberries," said Mrs. White. "And you still can't eat them!"

"Then how about a *date*?" asked the professor.

"I never date the guests," said Mrs. White. "But you're not hearing what I'm saying. This is fake fruit!"

"You mean it's just for decoration?" asked Miss Scarlet, twisting her ruby ring, which exactly matched the shade of her nail polish.

"Exactly," answered Mrs. White. "Mr. Boddy just bought it."

"Fake fruit?" asked Professor Plum.

Mrs. White nodded. "Each piece is actually glass — handmade by a famous artist named Honey Dew."

"Does this mean we won't be getting any dessert?" asked a disappointed Colonel Mustard.

"One thing at a time," pleaded Mrs. White. "I'll bring you all some milk and cookies in a little while."

The colonel stepped closer and examined the bowl of glass fruit. "Are they valuable?" he asked.

"Yes," admitted Mrs. White, "and if I see any

of you within ten feet of this fake fruit, I'll stew you like prunes. Mr. Boddy has asked me to keep a close eye on all of you."

The guests looked at one another and shrugged innocently. But each guest began to plot a way to steal the valuable glass fruit.

An hour later . . .

An hour later, after they had polished off some milk and cookies, the guests went their separate ways.

But soon, a guest sneaked back into the Lounge. Using the Rope as a lasso, she snagged the banana from the fruit bowl and dropped it in her purse. She rubbed one long, red fingernail along the valuable carved piece. "No one will miss one little old banana," she told herself as she walked away. "I better *peel* out of here before I slip up."

A few moments later, someone else entered the Lounge and took out the Knife. The guest carefully cut the wire stem of one purple grape, separated it from the cluster, popped it into a great hiding place — the mouth — and sneaked away.

Then a third guest entered and put a peach under his hat. "Oh, the peach fuzz tickles my head," he whispered to himself. But this guest was then surprised by a noise at the door. Turning, he saw Professor Plum, so he quickly pulled out the Revolver.

Professor Plum didn't see the Revolver and said pleasantly, "Hello, there. Now that I'm here, I'm not sure why I came."

He thought for a moment, then snapped his fingers. "Oh, yes," he said. "Mr. Green asked me to fetch him something. But I can't remember what exactly. I think it had something to do with vegetables, but I can't seem to remember!"

"Ah, vegetables," the guest with the Revolver said. "Mrs. White is putting out a nice vegetable tray in the Kitchen. Something for you and Mr. Green to *relish*."

"That Mrs. White is such a *peach*," said Professor Plum. "She's the *apple* of my eye."

"*Lettuce* — I mean, let us go together," suggested the guest. "Or, if you'd rather, we can race. I bet I can *beet* you there."

"You're so *corny*," laughed Plum. "Peas — I mean, *please*, let's *squash* these vegetable jokes before they start to *mushroom*."

"In that case, maybe you should go ahead to the Kitchen," the guest said, "and I'll *romaine* here."

"As you wish. I'll *leaf* you alone," Professor Plum said, and left the Lounge.

Then the guest with the grape in the mouth came back into the Lounge to steal again. But upon seeing the guest with the Revolver, the grape-stealer screamed, causing the grape to come shooting out onto the oriental rug. The glass grape rolled like a little purple marble and, luckily, didn't break.

Seeing the grape, the guest with the Revolver lunged for it. So did the guest with the Knife.

"Give me that grape!" one of them shouted.

"No, it's mine," the second replied. "Give it to me before I beat you to a pulp!"

"I saw it first," said the guest with the Revolver.

In the ensuing struggle, the peach fell out of its hiding place and rolled across the thick rug, too.

Then the guest with the stolen banana entered the Lounge and saw the struggle. "This is a prickly *pear* of a situation," she exclaimed. She also saw the grape and the peach on the rug. "All right, I'm in charge of the *currant* situation," she said. She took out her Rope and lassoed the guest with the Knife.

But the guest with the Revolver shouted, "Free that fruit or I'll shoot."

Unexpectedly, the Revolver went off and hit the silver bowl of fruit.

The remaining pieces of fruit shattered! Shards of glass flew in every direction.

"Now look what you have done!" said the guest with the Knife. "You've made fruit salad of Boddy's valuable sculpture!"

Suddenly, Mrs. White and Mr. Green appeared.

Mrs. White became as mad as a hornet. She said, "Professor Plum just warned me about this. When Mr. Boddy finds out, he'll use your head for banana bread!"

WHO SHOT THE BOWL OF FRUIT?

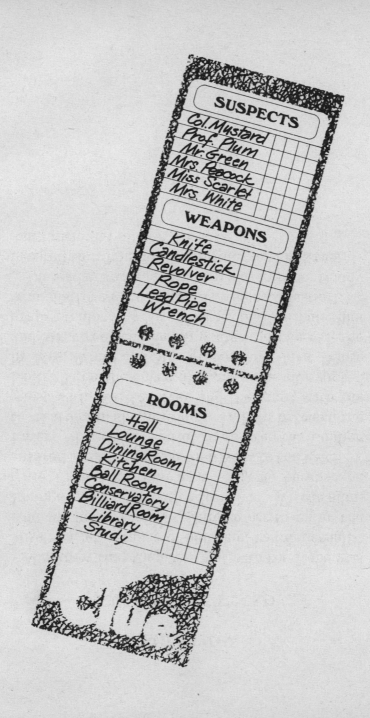

SOLUTION

COLONEL MUSTARD

We know that the first thief with the Rope was Miss Scarlet because of her long, red fingernails. And we know that the third guest to enter the Lounge was a male with a Revolver. We can eliminate Professor Plum as a suspect, because he entered the Lounge and then went to the Kitchen. Later, when Miss Scarlet re-entered the Lounge to steal again, she interrupted a fight between the guest with the Revolver and the guest with the Knife. Then the three of them were interrupted by Mrs. White and Mr. Green. Since Mrs. White and Mr. Green can be eliminated as suspects, the grape-stealer was Mrs. Peacock and the male thief who shattered the fruit was Colonel Mustard.

Instead of stewing Mustard like a prune, Boddy insisted that Mustard *eat* prunes for breakfast — and lunch and dinner, too.

5.
I'm So Board!

WHILE HIS GUESTS SLEPT, MR. BODDY went through the mansion and locked away all of his valuables. Needless to say, when his guests woke up and found what he had done, they were not pleased.

"The nerve of the man," said Colonel Mustard. "I'm challenging him to a duel. That is, once he unlocks his gold-handled dueling pistols."

"What are we to do if we can't steal Boddy's things?" asked a perplexed Mr. Green.

"You'd think he doesn't trust us," said a surprised Professor Plum.

"He says we're welcome to his mansion," Mrs. Peacock added, "but then not welcome to his things. The man's a hypocrite!"

When Mr. Boddy entered, the guests surrounded him.

"I'm so bored!" complained Miss Scarlet.

"Me too!" agreed Mr. Green.

"So am I," fussed Mrs. Peacock.

"Well," said Mr. Boddy, "as my dear mother used to say, 'Only boring people get bored.'"

"I'm not boring!" Mrs. Peacock protested. "How rude of you to suggest such a thing."

"Yes," added Colonel Mustard. "That sort of comment deserves a duel to the death!"

"Wait a minute, wait a minute," said Mr. Boddy. "Since you're all so bored, why don't you come outside and help me with the boards?"

"What boards?" asked Professor Plum. "Blackboards? I always write on the blackboard when I teach."

"And I use a cutting board in the kitchen," said Mrs. White.

"I use emery boards to file my nails," said Miss Scarlet.

"I have meetings in the boardroom," said Mr. Green.

"When I visit the ocean, I like to stroll on the boardwalk," said Mrs. Peacock.

"No," said Mr. Boddy, "I'm talking about boards for the new fence I'm building around my property."

"You want us to build a fence?" asked a shocked Miss Scarlet. "Why, that would ruin my nails."

"Yes," agreed Mrs. White. "And besides, it's hot outside."

"And your property covers acres and acres," moaned Mr. Green.

"And such hard work would give me aches and pains," said Mrs. Peacock, holding her back.

"And you're supposed to be entertaining us," complained Colonel Mustard.

"But I was thinking," said Mr. Boddy, "that you could divide up into two teams. And the team that nails up the most boards for the fence would get a very handsome reward."

"Like what?" asked Mr. Green.

"Hmmm," thought Mr. Boddy out loud. "How about a bucket of solid-gold nails? And a sterling-silver hammer for each member of the winning team?"

All the guests jumped at this opportunity.

Mrs. White began to sing, "If I had a hammer . . ."

"Nothing like pounding a few nails to get the heart racing," said Colonel Mustard.

"Actually, I read somewhere that hammering nails is good for the complexion," added Miss Scarlet.

"If properly done, there's nothing improper about building a fence," said Mrs. Peacock. "You know what they say: 'Good fences make good neighbors.'"

"Mr. Boddy, let me find my tool belt and I'll happily join in," said Professor Plum. He left the room, muttering, "Now where did I last see that tool belt?"

"Excellent!" boomed Mr. Boddy. "Let's meet outside in, say, ten minutes."

The guests agreed and raced to change into work clothes.

Ten minutes later . . .

Ten minutes later, the guests gathered on the mansion lawn.

"First, I need to separate you into two teams," said Mr. Boddy. "Team number 1 shall be Colonel Mustard, Mr. Green, and Mrs. Peacock."

"You mean we're stuck with the old bird?" Mr. Green whispered to Colonel Mustard.

Overhearing him, Mrs. Peacock waved her hammer and warned, "Better watch it, buster, before I knock some sense into you!"

"Better you knock a few nails," suggested Colonel Mustard.

Mr. Boddy continued, "Team number 2 is Mrs. White, Miss Scarlet, and Professor Plum."

Colonel Mustard laughed. "The absentminded professor and *two* ladies. We could beat you with one hand tied behind our backs!"

"Care to try it?" asked Miss Scarlet, taking out the Rope.

"Pay him no mind," advised Professor Plum. "Ladies, I have utmost confidence in our team."

"Wish I felt the same," Mrs. White said, eyeing the competition. "I'd like to nail them against the fence!"

"Ladies and gentlemen," Mr. Boddy said,

"allow me to explain the rules. The two teams will begin work on opposite ends of a twenty-foot section of fence poles. Please work your way toward the middle. Each side will have a large pile of fence boards and plenty of hammers and nails. You shall begin at my signal."

The teams separated. Team number 1 walked to one end of the twenty-foot section, and Team number 2 walked to the other end.

After each guest had selected a hammer and loaded up on nails, Mr. Boddy blew a whistle. "Go!" he shouted.

The two teams began furiously nailing up fence boards.

Colonel Mustard nailed up three boards.

Mrs. Peacock nailed up four boards.

Then Colonel Mustard nailed up two more and Mr. Green nailed one.

Mrs. White, working like a machine, nailed up eight, but two came loose and fell down.

Mr. Green added four more boards, and Mrs. Peacock added two.

Mrs. White, almost matching them nail for nail, put up five more boards. "Come on!" she shouted at Professor Plum. "Why haven't you started yet?"

"I lost my hammer," Professor Plum said. "Have you seen it?"

"It's in your hand, you fool!" shouted Miss Scarlet, nailing up a board.

"Ah, so it is." Quickly catching up, Professor Plum nailed up a rush of boards. When he had finished, his team was leading by five.

Miss Scarlet nailed one more for her team. But then she suddenly stopped.

"What's the matter?" asked Mrs. White.

"I broke a nail," moaned Miss Scarlet.

"There's plenty more in the bucket," Mrs. White told her.

"A *fingernail*," explained Miss Scarlet. "This is a serious injury."

"Oh, come now!" said Professor Plum.

"You don't understand," said Miss Scarlet. "My manicurist is on vacation until next week!"

"Get back to work," Mrs. White warned, "or you'll have more than a fingernail to worry about!"

Then Mr. Green "accidentally" knocked one of Mrs. White's boards down.

"Hey, that's not fair!" she protested.

So she retaliated by bumping into Mrs. Peacock while she was nailing, and Peacock's team lost two boards.

"It's rude to bump into someone and then not apologize!" said Mrs. Peacock. "I'm quite displeased with you."

"I'm so scared," sneered Mrs. White.

Colonel Mustard's hammer somehow flew from his hand, shot through the air, and knocked down four boards, just nailed up by Miss Scarlet.

"Colonel, you did that on purpose!" shouted Miss Scarlet.

"This is getting much too dangerous," complained Professor Plum. "Besides, I'm dying of thirst." So he took a break for lemonade, during which time Mr. Green nailed two new boards and Mrs. Peacock added three.

Working like a woman possessed, Mrs. Peacock nailed three more for her team. "I haven't had this much fun," she said, "since I taught a class of fourth-graders the proper way to curtsy."

"You're almost done," shouted Mr. Boddy, watching the progress.

With a final burst of energy, Miss Scarlet nailed three new boards, and Mrs. White nailed up four.

Finally, the two teams met in the middle and Mr. Boddy blew the whistle.

WHO WON THE CONTEST?

HOW MANY BOARDS DID EACH TEAM NAIL?

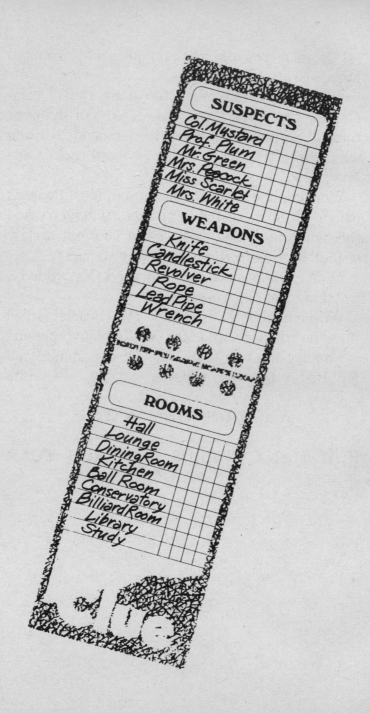

SOLUTION

TEAM NUMBER 2 wins with 28 boards.
TEAM NUMBER 1 nailed 22 boards.

By keeping track of the members of each team and the simple addition and subtraction, the solution is "above board." But since Boddy decided that each team's behavior was "board-ering" on unfair, no one was awarded the golden nails and silver hammers.

6.
Saved by the Radio

THE GUESTS WERE ENJOYING AN UN-
usually quiet time in the Conservatory. Miss Scarlet had beaten Professor Plum three straight
times at chess. Mrs. White was relaxing by ar-
ranging freshly cut flowers in a vase. Mr. Green
happily made stacks with the pretend money
from one of Mr. Boddy's board games. And
Mrs. Peacock sat by the window, embroidering a
doily.

Colonel Mustard entered. He had been in his
room, polishing his dueling pistols. "Well, isn't
this the picture of contentment," he said to himself. "Time to put a little life into this crowd."

He strode over to Mr. Boddy's antique radio
and turned it to his favorite station. Then he ad-
justed the volume until it was quite loud. Military
marching music blared into the previously peace-
ful room.

"Turn down that racket!" shouted Mr. Green.

"Never! I love this music!" replied Colonel Mustard. He began to march around the room, using
the Lead Pipe as a pretend bugle. "Nothing like

the sound of drums and brass to get my blood racing."

"Why don't you and your blood and your music race right out of here?" suggested Mrs. White.

But the marching music was too loud, and Colonel Mustard didn't hear. "Putting on my dress uniform. Polishing my shoes and swords. Pinning on the best of my medals. Marching shoulder to shoulder with my fellow soldiers. This music reminds me of the good old days in the war," he said.

"There will be a war in this room if you don't turn it off," warned Mr. Green.

To prove his point, Mr. Green got up and turned the radio to *his* favorite station.

The sound of New Orleans jazz replaced the marching music. "Ah, the French Quarter of New Orleans," mused Mr. Green. "Dixieland bands and great Cajun cooking. The Mardi Gras parade and a streetcar named Desire."

"A streetcar named Desire?" asked Professor Plum. "That's the silliest thing I've ever heard of."

"New Orleans was the cradle of jazz," said Mr. Green. He began using the Wrench to pantomime playing a clarinet.

"I think jazz is rude," stated Mrs. Peacock, waving her Candlestick for attention. "And rock and roll is even more rude. There's only one kind of music I like."

"Let me guess," sneered Miss Scarlet. "The only kind of music you like is — no music."

"Appreciating good music shows one's breeding," said Mrs. Peacock. "And the only music worth appreciating was written by the likes of Beethoven, Bach, and Mozart!"

But before she could get to the radio, another person got up and changed the station. The jazz was replaced by country music. And the person who changed the station began making a lasso with the Rope and shouting, "I always wanted to be a cowboy!"

"Because you like to ride wild horses and herd cows?" asked Colonel Mustard.

"No, because there's never a maid in a Western movie," the person said. She began doing a Texas two-step to the twangy beat.

"That's disgusting, Mrs. White," said yet another guest, who changed the station. "I hate country music but I love *this*."

A new type of music altogether filled the room and the person who had changed the station began dancing and shaking her hair.

"Stop! Please stop!" screamed Mrs. Peacock. "I told you that's the other type of music I find rude."

"Yes," agreed a second party, pointing a Knife. "It's too loud, and I haven't had a chance to hear my favorite station, yet."

"Wait just a moment," interrupted Mr. Boddy, entering the room. "Instead of fighting over the radio station like a roomful of children, why don't you each go to a different room in the mansion?"

"It sounds like you're treating us like children and sending us to our rooms," said Colonel Mustard.

"I'm only trying to accommodate all of your varied tastes," explained Mr. Boddy.

"Well, I'm not leaving unless I can march out of here to my own music," insisted Colonel Mustard.

"Please be reasonable," said Mr. Boddy. "Surely you know by now that each room in my mansion has its own separate radio — except for the Hall, Dining Room, and Ball Room.

"But this radio sounds the best," said Mr. Green. "I'm not leaving, either."

"Nor I," added Mrs. Peacock.

"I was afraid this might happen," said Mr. Boddy. "I hate to do this, but to make sure there's no trouble, I'll just hold on to the Revolver." To show the guests he meant business, he removed it from his pocket.

"In that case, I'll be happy to depart," said Miss Scarlet.

"Wait for me," said Professor Plum.

"A radio for each one of us is a brilliant solution, sir," said Colonel Mustard. He, too, left.

"Yes, yes, leave it to Mr. Boddy," said Mrs. White, heading for the door.

Mr. Green and Mrs. Peacock soon followed.

In the Hall, the guests went their own ways.

Soon, the mansion was filled with the sounds of six different radio stations blaring six different programs.

In the room full of books, the guest with the Lead Pipe began marching around the room. "Spines straight! Stay in line!" he ordered the books.

In another room, someone climbed on a green felt table and danced to loud music. She used a cue stick as a pretend microphone.

From the Lounge wafted the sounds of classical music.

In the room with the cooking stove someone pantomimed the clarinet.

In another room, a guest listened closely to the radio there.

In the original room where everyone first gathered, someone practiced roping cows.

Ten minutes later . . .

Ten minutes later, a guest emerged and raced to the front Hall. There the guest called loudly for all to hear, "There's a thunderstorm warning effective immediately. We must shut all the windows!"

Mr. Boddy and the others came running.

"A bad storm is heading our way," the guest repeated.

"Everyone, please help," said Mr. Boddy. "Mr. Green, Mrs. Peacock, come with me to shut the upstairs windows. Mrs. White, you and Professor Plum make certain all the main-floor windows are closed. Colonel Mustard, check the doors. And Miss Scarlet, just in case, find some candles and blankets."

Everyone rushed into action.

After the mansion had been secured for bad weather, Mr. Boddy congratulated his guest for warning the others and saving the mansion from getting drenched.

"Well," beamed the proud guest, "it helps when your favorite program is the news and weather station."

WHICH GUEST, WITH WHICH WEAPON, IN WHICH ROOM, WARNED THE OTHERS OF THE STORM?

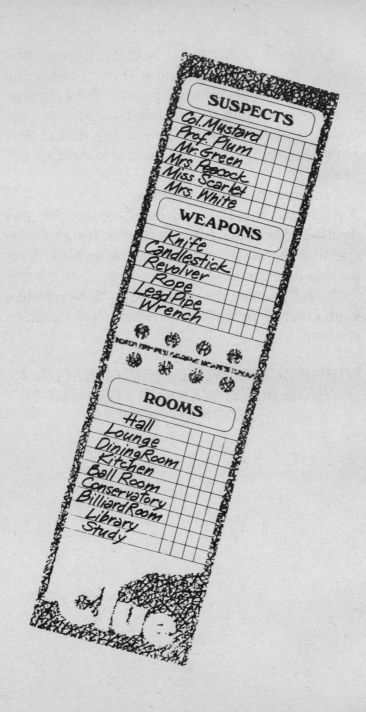

SOLUTION

PROFESSOR PLUM with the KNIFE in the STUDY

We can eliminate Colonel Mustard and Mr. Green because we learn early on that they listen to marching music and jazz. We learn that Mrs. Peacock hates jazz and rock and roll, but likes classical music. Then Mrs. White is identified by name as liking country music. Finally, we discover that Miss Scarlet is the person who likes to dance to rock and roll.

This leaves only Professor Plum with an unidentified radio station preference, so he is the guest who listens to the news and weather station. We know he had the Knife, because earlier he was holding it while complaining that he was the only guest who didn't get to listen to his program. We know he was in the Study because all the other rooms with radios have been eliminated.

A proud Mr. Boddy told Professor Plum that in honor of him, everyone would listen to *his* station all weekend long. And it was a *long* weekend.

7.
The Midnight Snack Death

AT MR. BODDY'S REQUEST, MRS. WHITE prepared a most unusual meal. Everything she served that night was an animal body part.

"How clever," said Miss Scarlet.

"Well, I find the theme quite rude," commented Mrs. Peacock. "Sometimes our host has the strangest sense of humor."

"Mankind has been eating the parts of animals since we all lived in caves," observed Colonel Mustard. "It's part of nature."

"I'm sure we're in for a first-rate dining experience," said Mr. Green.

When Mrs. White rang the dinner bell, the guests rushed into the Dining Room and took their seats.

The appetizers included chopped goose livers and barbecued chicken wings. The soup was made with oxtails. The salad contained pickled pig's knuckles. And the entree was a choice of leg of lamb, kidney pie, or tongue sandwiches.

"Good thing Old McDonald isn't here," whispered Miss Scarlet, forcing down a bite. "Because we're being served every animal on his farm."

"What isn't overcooked is undercooked. Mrs. White, I can't eat this lamb," complained Mr. Green.

"And why not?" asked Mrs. White.

"Because I think it just *baahed*!"

"And I swear my tongue sandwich is still *mooing*," added Mrs. Peacock.

"Dare I ask what's for dessert?" asked Professor Plum.

"I was planning on ladyfingers," said Mrs. White sarcastically.

Colonel Mustard pushed his plate away. "I think I just lost my appetite," he said.

"I lost mine the moment I saw a real oxtail floating in my soup," said Professor Plum.

"Mrs. White, what happened?" asked Green. "You'd think you had the brains of a sheep!"

"I did have the brains of a sheep," said Mrs. White, "until I threw them in the salad."

Mrs. Peacock quickly covered her mouth with a napkin. She moaned, "This may be the most disgusting meal I've ever had the *dish*-pleasure of eating."

Suddenly Miss Scarlet stopped eating. "I haven't seen Mr. Boddy's cat all afternoon," she noted. A sickening look came over her face. She turned to the maid and said, "Mrs. White, you wouldn't have . . . ?"

Mrs. White smiled slyly. "That's for me to know and you to find out," she said.

"That's it!" Colonel Mustard said. He stood up and furiously threw his napkin to the table. "I'd rather starve than eat another bite."

"Suit yourself," said Mrs. White. "But I'm not preparing another thing. The Kitchen is closed!"

"What a fine time to start my latest diet," said Miss Scarlet. She excused herself and left the table.

"I wasn't all that hungry to begin with," said Professor Plum, joining her.

"Wait for me," called Mr. Green, who looked a little green.

"Mrs. Peacock, aren't you leaving like the others?" asked Mrs. White.

"Yes," Mrs. Peacock said. "Mrs. White, you should be ashamed!"

Later that evening . . .

Later that evening, Mr. Green sneaked into the Kitchen. Not wasting a moment, he opened the refrigerator and began to raid it. "Let's see," he said, "this cheese looks good. Here's some bread, lettuce, tomatoes, and pickles." Happily, he began to make himself a sandwich.

Soon he was interrupted by Miss Scarlet.

"I didn't touch a bite of Mrs. White's disgusting

dinner. I'm so hungry I could eat a horse," she exclaimed.

"Careful," warned Mr. Green, "or a horse is exactly what will be on tomorrow night's dinner menu!"

"What did you find to eat?" she asked.

"I'm making myself a deli sandwich," said Mr. Green. "I'd be happy to make one for you, too."

"No, thank you." She opened the freezer. "Now, here's something that looks good." She removed a container of fat-free frozen yogurt.

In a little while, they were joined by Professor Plum. "Ah, I'm not the only one who couldn't stomach Mrs. White's dreadful cooking," he observed. "That woman should be shot!"

"Splendid idea!" Mr. Green said, taking a big bite out of his sandwich.

"Yes, yes," Miss Scarlet chuckled, digging a spoon into her frozen yogurt.

Colonel Mustard entered. "I see some other guests are as hungry as I." He happily reheated what was left of the previous day's lunch. "The service at this place has gone downhill in a hurry," he complained. "If I wasn't here as Boddy's guest, I'd challenge him to a duel!"

"It wasn't Boddy doing the cooking," Miss Scarlet reminded him. "It was Mrs. White!"

"Yes, someone should strangle that woman!" Colonel Mustard said.

To no one's surprise, Mrs. Peacock soon joined them in the Kitchen.

"Hello, everyone," she said. "Please allow me to join the midnight snacking. Normally it's very poor manners to raid the refrigerator, but after today's dinner, no one would blame us if we raided a grocery store!"

"An awful, awful meal," said Professor Plum. "We were just saying that someone should take care of Mrs. White!"

"Hit her over the head with a blunt instrument," Mrs. Peacock suggested, munching on a cold turkey drumstick. "A Wrench, for instance, or a Lead Pipe!"

"Or a Candlestick!" added Miss Scarlet. "That would be a blow to her ego!"

Suddenly they were interrupted by Mrs. White. "I was in the Conservatory," she explained, "doing a little late-night cleaning to calm my nerves. I was coming here to refill my bucket of sudsy water — when I overheard your fiendish plotting!"

"We were just kidding, my dear," said Mr. Green, taking the last bite of his sandwich. "No harm will come to you."

"It had better not," warned Mrs. White, "or I might serve one of you as the main course one night!"

"How rude!" said Mrs. Peacock.

Mr. Green took his plate to the sink. "Good

night, all," he said. "I'm off to the Library to find some bedtime reading."

"I'll go with you," said Colonel Mustard.

While Mrs. White refilled her bucket with sudsy water, Mrs. Peacock and Miss Scarlet finished their snacks.

"Good night," said Mrs. Peacock.

"Aren't you going to say something?" Mrs. White asked Miss Scarlet.

Miss Scarlet shook her head.

"How come?" asked Mrs. White with a menacing smile. "Cat got your tongue?"

Miss Scarlet stomped her feet and left. She joined Mrs. Peacock in the Hall and they headed upstairs together, leaving Professor Plum alone with Mrs. White.

"Do you think my life is in danger?" she asked him.

"Who would kill the cook just because she made the worst dinner in history?" he responded. "I imagine you're as exhausted as I am and looking forward to a good night's sleep."

Mrs. White looked around the Kitchen. "First I have to deal with the latest mess you and the other guests made in here. Then I still have to sweep up the trash left in the Ball Room from this afternoon's tango contest."

"Well, sweet dreams," said Professor Plum. He, too, headed upstairs.

Later that night, one of the guests, holding the Revolver, checked in Mrs. Peacock's room and found her sound asleep.

The guest crept down the stairs and stopped outside of the Library, hearing a pair of voices arguing from inside.

One voice said, "I had that book first! It's my favorite!"

The other voice replied, "No, you didn't! Green, give it back this instant — or I'll challenge you to a duel!"

The guest tiptoed past the Library door.

The guest walked purposefully to the Kitchen, strode in, and aimed the Revolver. "Here's your just desserts, Mrs. White!" the guest said.

But the Kitchen was empty.

"Where is she?" the guest asked.

After a frantic search of the mansion's other rooms, the guest found Mrs. White and said, "If you thought your cooking was bad, try a taste of this."

With that, the guest murdered poor Mrs. White.

WHO MURDERED MRS. WHITE?

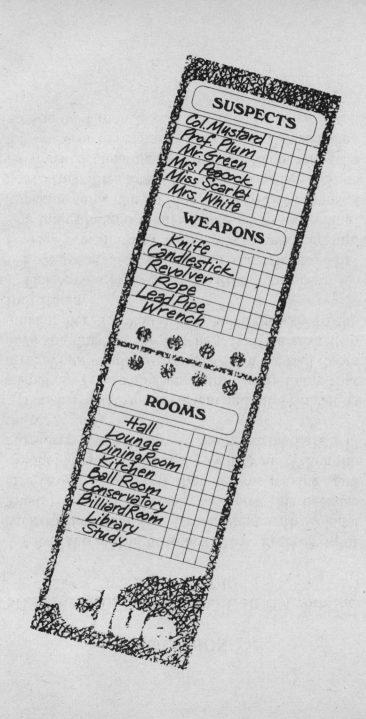

SOLUTION

MISS SCARLET in the BALL ROOM with the REVOLVER

After the midnight snack, Mrs. Peacock went back to bed, and Mr. Green went with Colonel Mustard to the Library. We know this because Mr. Green announced that he was leaving, and Colonel Mustard said "I'll go with you." When the murderer walks by later, the gentlemen are still there.

This leaves Professor Plum and Miss Scarlet as suspects. Yet Professor Plum clearly knew that Mrs. White would be going to clean the Ball Room once she finished the Kitchen. So if he wished to murder her, he would have gone directly to the Ball Room.

This leaves Miss Scarlet as the murderer. Fortunately, as she pulled the trigger, Miss Scarlet was doubled over by a stomach cramp. The bullet lodged itself harmlessly in the ceiling, knocking some plaster loose. Mrs. White promised not to turn Miss Scarlet over to the police if Scarlet finished cleaning up the Ball Room and paid for a caterer to prepare every meal in the mansion for the next month.

8.
Hats Off!

Mr. BODDY INVITED HIS GUESTS INTO the Conservatory, where he had arranged six round boxes in a semicircle.

"What's Boddy up to this time?" asked Miss Scarlet. "Is he showing off his odd-shaped box collection?"

"Is this some sort of game?" asked Mr. Green. "Are we supposed to jump from box to box like frogs leaping lily pads?"

"No one's to touch these boxes but I," ordered Mr. Boddy. "What's inside is very fragile. And very valuable."

"Maybe the boxes contain a collection of the crown jewels of Europe," said a hopeful Mrs. Peacock.

"Or a collection of diamond-studded belts," guessed Colonel Mustard.

"I've long suspected Boddy of having a set of sterling-silver serving plates," said Mrs. White. "Plates too valuable to actually use, but worth a fortune to any serious collector."

"I'm hoping it's a set of the largest gold coins ever minted," stated Mr. Green. "If it is," he then whispered to himself, "I'll be the first to steal them."

"Professor Plum, we haven't heard from you yet," observed Mr. Boddy. "You have a faraway look in your eye. Like your mind is elsewhere."

"His mind is *always* elsewhere," whispered Mrs. White.

After a minute of serious contemplation, Professor Plum offered his prediction. "Mr. Boddy, being a sports fan, I bet you are about to show us a set of antique discuses from the first Olympics in Ancient Greece."

"I'm sorry, Professor, but I'll have to toss your best guess out. Ladies and gentlemen, I've yet to hear the correct speculation," said Mr. Boddy.

"Then give us a hint," suggested Miss Scarlet.

"Very well. I have the topper of all my possessions to share with you," Mr. Boddy said.

"You call that a hint?" said an irritated Mrs. Peacock.

"Now I'm more confused than ever," said Professor Plum.

"No surprise there," Mr. Green whispered to Mrs. White.

"Boddy, have you flipped your lid?" sneered Colonel Mustard.

"If Mr. Boddy has something valuable to show

us, we'd best hold onto our hats," advised Professor Plum.

"Exactly!" Mr. Boddy said, to his guests' bewilderment.

"My good man," said Colonel Mustard, "I don't know what you're hiding under your hat. But you best show it to us this instant before I lose my temper and challenge you to a duel."

"I quite agree," added Mrs. Peacock.

Mr. Boddy opened the first box and removed a delicate golden headpiece.

"I hope you're not planning on passing the hat to pay for our visit," said Mr. Green.

"Actually, this belonged to Cleopatra, Queen of the Nile," said Mr. Boddy. "As you can see, it's made of real gold, with silver thread and tiny jewels. It's over two thousand years old."

"No wonder she wanted to get rid of it," whispered Miss Scarlet. "Personally, I never wear anything that's more than a week old."

"Since this headpiece once belonged to a regal woman, I think you, Mrs. Peacock, should try it on," said Mr. Boddy.

"Why, how sweet," cooed Mrs. Peacock. She carefully put it on. "How do I look?" she asked.

"I can close my eyes and see you riding on a slow barge up the Nile," kidded Colonel Mustard.

Mr. Boddy opened the second box and removed

a large felt hat with a full, turned-up brim. He handed it to Colonel Mustard, who tried it on.

"Definitely a military hat," Colonel Mustard said, pulling it down snugly.

"Right," Mr. Boddy said. "That hat belonged to Napoléon Bonaparte, the great French general who met his match at Waterloo."

"The Battle of Waterloo cut poor Napoléon down to size," added Professor Plum.

"Looking at that silly hat, I can see why he lost," observed Miss Scarlet.

" 'Nappy' was one of the greatest military minds of all time," insisted Colonel Mustard. "You take back that insult this instant!"

"His military mind may have been great," conceded Miss Scarlet, "but I wouldn't lose my head over his sense of fashion."

"I see that you're itching for the next hat," Mr. Boddy said to the professor. He opened the third box and removed a tall stovepipe hat. "This belonged to Abraham Lincoln. He was wearing it when he gave the Gettysburg Address."

Professor Plum tried it on. "Which house was Lincoln looking for in Gettysburg?" he asked.

"Beg your pardon?" said Mr. Boddy.

"The address?" asked Professor Plum.

"The Gettysburg Address was a speech, you fool!" said Mr. Green.

"I hate to be a bother, but I don't like Napoléon's hat," Colonel Mustard said. "It's giving me a complex." So he traded hats with Professor Plum.

"Here's something you may like," Mr. Boddy told Miss Scarlet as he opened the fourth round box. He removed a white ermine hat. "This was worn by Queen Elizabeth of England."

"Now there's a woman with good taste!" Miss Scarlet eagerly tried it on. "But it's too small!"

"Then trade with me," urged Mrs. Peacock.

"But your hat is too old," whined Miss Scarlet.

"I'll take yours," Mrs. White said to Miss Scarlet.

The fifth hatbox contained a derby once worn by the great silent movie clown Charlie Chaplin. Boddy presented it to Mr. Green.

"Look how it falls over my ears," complained Mr. Green. "It's much too big."

"It's good for a laugh," said Mrs. Peacock. "Maybe that's why Charlie Chaplin wore it."

"People will think I can't afford the right size," said Mr. Green, and he traded hats with Professor Plum.

The last box held a brand-new leopard-skin pillbox hat. "This belonged to my mother. She wore it when she and my father celebrated their fiftieth wedding anniversary," Mr. Boddy said with a tear in his eye.

He gave it to the one guest still needing something atop her head.

While Mr. Boddy was putting the boxes away,

Mrs. Peacock eyed the hat that Mrs. White had on. "I hate to be ungrateful," she told Mr. Boddy, "but I much prefer that one."

"Mrs. White, would you mind trading?" asked Mr. Boddy.

"Fine by me," Mrs. White said.

So the women traded.

"I don't particularly wish to be in a man's shoes," Miss Scarlet said, "but I've always been curious how I might look wearing a man's style of hat."

"Here's your chance," said Mr. Green, trading with her.

"As long as we're each wearing different hats," Professor Plum said, "is someone willing to trade with me?"

"I will," said Mrs. White.

But Mr. Green was still not happy. So, when Colonel Mustard wasn't watching, Mr. Green switched hats with him.

"Some of you look, well, awfully silly," insisted Mr. Boddy. "Colonel, please trade hats with Miss Scarlet."

They did so.

Even so, Boddy was not finished. "Mrs. Peacock," he said, "you and Mrs. White do the same."

"But Mr. Boddy — " began Mrs. Peacock.

"Please do as I say," insisted Mr. Boddy.

A glum Mrs. Peacock traded hats with Mrs. White.

"I'm beginning to feel like a hat rack," joked Mrs. White.

"There," said a pleased Mr. Boddy. "This would make a perfect picture."

WHO IS WEARING WHICH HAT?

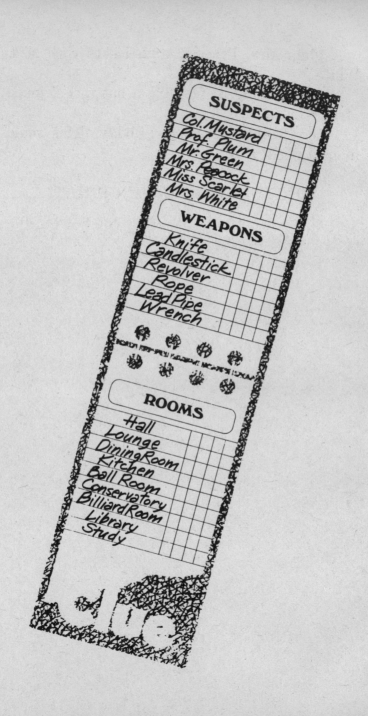

SOLUTION

MR. GREEN is wearing Lincoln's stovepipe hat, COLONEL MUSTARD has Napoleon's felt hat, MRS. PEACOCK has Chaplin's derby, MISS SCARLET has the pillbox once worn by Boddy's mother, MRS. WHITE has Queen Elizabeth's white ermine hat, and PROFESSOR PLUM has Cleopatra's headpiece.

The first switch was between Colonel Mustard and Professor Plum. Then Mrs. White and Miss Scarlet traded. Mr. Green traded the derby for Napoleon's hat, which Professor Plum temporarily had. Since Miss Scarlet remained hatless, she got the leopard-skin pillbox hat. At her request, Mrs. Peacock traded with Mrs. White, taking the ermine, leaving Mrs. White with Cleo's golden headgear. Miss Scarlet and Mr. Green traded. Professor Plum and Mrs. White traded. Mr. Green switched the pillbox hat for Colonel Mustard's stovepipe one when the colonel wasn't looking. Finally, Colonel Mustard gave Miss Scarlet back the pillbox hat, and reclaimed the general's felt style, while Mrs. Peacock ended up with the derby and Mrs. White got the white ermine hat. Before they could stop him, Mr. Boddy snapped a picture of his silly guests. He threatened to print it in the newspaper the next time they misbehaved.

9.
In the Swim

THE MANSION AND THE SURROUNDING countryside were in the midst of a heat wave. Everyone was feeling the effects of the unseasonably hot weather.

"I haven't been this hot since my days marching through the jungle," said Colonel Mustard. He took a handkerchief and wiped his brow.

"An unseasonable warming trend like this is caused by unusual sunspot activity," said Professor Plum. "At least, that's one theory."

"Theory or no theory, we're running low on lemonade and iced tea," said Mrs. White.

"I told Mr. Boddy years ago to invest in some air-conditioning," said an angry Mr. Green. "But he said the mansion didn't need it because it's so well insulated. Well, I think it's Boddy's skull that is so well insulated!"

"It's rude to blame our host for the weather," scolded Mrs. Peacock. She had made no concession to the heat. In fact, she was dressed in an ankle-length gown with full sleeves.

"Aren't you awfully sweaty in that outfit?" Miss Scarlet asked.

"A proper lady never sweats," observed Mrs. Peacock. "Nor does she wear a flimsy, sleeveless dress like yours."

"To each her own," said Miss Scarlet, fanning herself with a rolled-up fashion magazine. "Besides, it's too warm to argue."

Professor Plum took a moment to observe the tropical fish swimming in Boddy's enormous glass tank. "It must be extraordinarily hot," he observed, "because it appears even Mr. Boddy's fish are sweating!"

Mr. Boddy entered and found his guests hot and unhappy. "You know," he said, "the basement is the coolest place in the mansion. We could all go down there."

"Too musty," said Mrs. Peacock.

"Too dark," added Professor Plum.

"Too dusty," stated Miss Scarlet.

"Too dank," added Mr. Green.

"You should try to keep this place clean by yourselves!" said a wounded Mrs. White.

"We could pile into one of my cars and go for a drive," suggested Mr. Boddy.

"Too crowded," said Miss Scarlet.

"Too windy," remarked Professor Plum.

"Too fast," stated Mrs. Peacock.

"Too slow," added Mr. Green.

"Colonel, don't you have an opinion?" asked Mr. Boddy.

"It's too hot for an opinion," said a panting Colonel Mustard. "It's even too hot for dueling!"

Mr. Boddy thought for a moment. "I've got it!" he said excitedly. "I'll open my Olympic-size swimming pool."

"What a great idea. Something else for me to clean," muttered Mrs. White.

"I don't mind," Miss Scarlet said, "as long as I don't have to get wet. Give me a comfortable lounge chair, a cool drink, a good book, and the chance to work on my tan — and I'll be happy."

"You're right about pools," said Professor Plum. "Water *is* such a nuisance sometimes. I think someone should invent a waterless swimming pool."

"Given the way his mind works at times," joked Mrs. White, "I think that Plum once dived into a waterless pool!"

"You can count me out," said Mrs. Peacock. "The thought of seeing each and every one of you wearing a swimsuit — it's uncivilized!"

"The truth is," Colonel Mustard replied, "that you, Mrs. Peacock, wouldn't be caught dead wearing something as brief as a swimsuit!"

"Imagine Peacock in the water," said Mr. Green. The thought made him chuckle.

"Sir, I'll have you know that I loved to swim as a girl," retorted Mrs. Peacock.

"I didn't realize that water had been invented when you were a girl," kidded Miss Scarlet.

"How rude!" said Mrs. Peacock.

"Ladies and gentlemen, you're getting overheated," warned Mr. Boddy. "A dip in a nice, big swimming pool should cool you off."

"I'll be first off the diving board," bragged Colonel Mustard. "You should see my cannonball!"

"Splashing is a show of bad manners," stated Mrs. Peacock. "The only proper thing to do off a diving board is the swan dive. I was also an excellent diver as a girl."

"So Peacock was a young swan?" asked a confused Professor Plum.

"Can we continue this discussion at the pool?" Mr. Boddy asked.

It was such a hot day that everyone agreed.

"Don't forget to coat your exposed skin with sunblock," advised Mr. Boddy. "We don't want anyone suffering from a bad case of sunburn." He checked his watch. "Let's meet outside at the pool in, say, twenty minutes."

Slowly, so as not to exert themselves, the guests walked to their rooms and changed into their swimsuits.

Twenty minutes later . . .

Twenty minutes later, everyone met by the pool.

91

To no one's surprise, Mr. Green was wearing a green swimsuit, Colonel Mustard a yellow, and Professor Plum a purple.

The women were wearing black swimsuits with large polka dots: Mrs. White's polka dots were white, Miss Scarlet's were red, and Mrs. Peacock's were blue.

"Doesn't the water look inviting?" asked Mrs. Peacock.

"It certainly does," said Professor Plum.

Miss Scarlet put the tip of her red-painted toenail in the water. "Ummm," she said, "the temperature is just right."

"Then it's too warm for me," complained Colonel Mustard. "I'm used to swimming in a bone-chilling lake. Nothing like a bracing dip to wake a person up."

"Then why don't you go jump in a lake?" suggested Mrs. White.

"And I like my water as hot as a hot tub," complained Mr. Green. "Nothing like a good soak in a hot tub after a long day making oceans of money."

"Yes, you should go soak your head," sneered Miss Scarlet.

Mr. Boddy walked to the end of the diving board to test the bounce. He was still dressed in his suit and tie. He hopped up and down several times.

"Just right!" he claimed. "Who will be the first to give it a try?"

But just then, Mr. Boddy lost his balance and fell right into the water! *Kerr-splash!*

"Help him!" screamed Mrs. White. "Someone help! He doesn't know how to swim!"

"Then it's time he learned!" said an unfeeling Mr. Green.

"I'll take care of it," said the guest in the yellow swimsuit, diving right in.

"No, I'll take care of it," said a guest in a polka-dot swimsuit, jumping in as well.

But the two guests bumped heads in the water.

"Now I'll have to save all three," said Mr. Green. "And afterwards I'll charge them a pretty penny for having done so!"

"You'll be in over your head," said Mrs. White.

"I will be in a moment," said Mr. Green, jumping in while holding his nose.

But Mr. Green misjudged his jump and sank all the way to the bottom of the pool. There he pushed off with both legs and shot back to the surface. When he emerged, he swallowed a mouthful of water and couldn't help the others.

"This is horrible!" shouted the guest who was wearing the red polka dots. "What should we do?"

"We could stand here and watch them drown," suggested Mrs. White.

"You can't be serious!" said the guest. So she dashed to the pool house, where she found a large, inflated rubber raft.

Taking it by its rope handle, she squeezed the

raft through the door. But, rushing toward the pool, the rope on the raft caught her foot and she fell in the pool, too.

The raft went soaring into the air and landed in the deep end.

Luckily, Mr. Boddy, Colonel Mustard, and one of the women grabbed the raft and hung on for dear life.

But when another male guest tried to reach the raft, he lost his breath and began to sink. "Help me!" he cried with his last gasp.

To his great fortune, the man not on the raft was saved by a guest who lay down on the deck and held out the Candlestick. "Grab hold!"

The floundering guest in the water managed to grab the end of the Candlestick. But, in doing so, he accidentally pulled his rescuer into the water.

So another person raced to the pool house and found a second raft. Holding the raft high overhead, this person raced to the edge of the pool and jumped in to help.

WHO WAS NOT IN THE WATER?

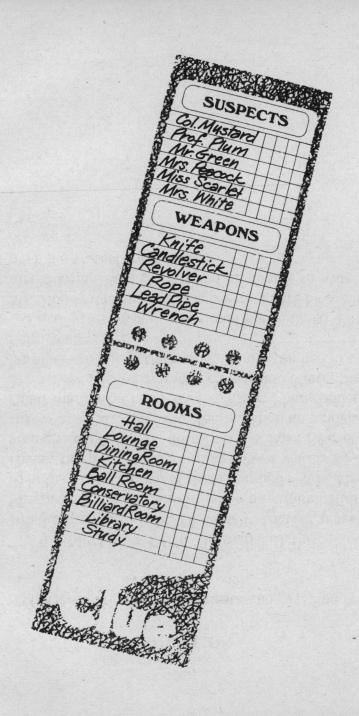

SOLUTION

NO ONE. All six of the guests and Mr. Boddy were in the pool.

After Mr. Boddy fell in, the man with the yellow suit jumped in to help. Obviously, this is Colonel Mustard. Then an unidentified woman jumped in to help. After the two of them bumped heads, Mr. Green jumped in. But he swallowed water, so a woman in red polka dots, who is Miss Scarlet, threw in a raft. She, too, fell in. Then an unidentified man, who must be Professor Plum, pulled Mr. Green to the edge but fell in. Mrs. White, the only person not in the water, finally jumped in to help, too.

Luckily, everyone was saved and unhurt. But Mr. Boddy decided to drain the pool until he could hire a large team of qualified lifeguards to watch over his waterlogged guests.

10.
Death by Candlelight

IT WAS THE GUESTS' LAST EVENING IN the mansion.

"I hate leaving so soon," said a saddened Mrs. Peacock. "Especially before I've had the chance to steal something truly valuable."

"I know how you feel," said Mr. Green. "I despise leaving and not being any richer than when I arrived."

"I suppose it was fun enough," added Colonel Mustard. "Considering I wasn't able to enjoy a single duel all weekend."

Miss Scarlet had a tear in her eye.

"I know it isn't from dust," said Mrs. White. "Because I've been cleaning every minute since the lot of you arrived!"

"It's a tear of despair," said Miss Scarlet.

"You're sad to be leaving tomorrow?" asked Professor Plum.

"No," Miss Scarlet said. "I'm sad that there are still a few outfits I didn't get to wear this weekend."

"Cheer up," Colonel Mustard said. "I bet we'll be back for another visit."

"Because we're such good friends to Mr. Boddy?" asked Mr. Green.

"No," corrected Colonel Mustard. "Because there's a lot more for us to walk away with."

" 'Parting is such sweet sorrow,' " quoted Professor Plum.

"What does that mean?" asked Mrs. White.

"I have no idea," admitted Professor Plum. "But if it was good enough for William Shakespeare, it's good enough for me!"

Later, after a lavish farewell dinner, Mr. Boddy called his guests into the Library. They were seated in plush reading chairs and served tea.

"Are you going to read us a good-bye story?" asked Colonel Mustard, looking over the huge collection of books.

"There's *A Farewell to Arms*," suggested Professor Plum. "And *Goodbye, Mr. Chips*."

"I didn't call you here to read to you," said Mr. Boddy.

"Thank goodness," whispered Miss Scarlet. "I hate how he insists on doing all of the characters' different voices."

"Then state your business," said Mr. Green. "Remember, time is money."

"Very well," said Mr. Boddy. "I realize that, although you guests are my dearest friends, strange things have been known to happen during your visits here."

"Only about every five minutes," Mrs. White whispered to herself.

"Valuables suddenly disappear," Mr. Boddy went on, "and lives are threatened."

"Now, see here!" protested Colonel Mustard. "Any man who spreads such lies — I challenge you to a duel to the death this instant!"

"My point exactly," Mr. Boddy sadly observed.

"And this poppycock about our being thieves!" stormed Mr. Green. "Nothing could be further from the truth! Mr. Boddy, it makes me very, very, very sad to hear in what low esteem you hold us."

Mr. Green reached into his pocket for a handkerchief with which to wipe the tears from his eyes — and accidentally dropped one of Boddy's priceless diamond stickpins.

"Green, my stickpin!" Mr. Boddy shouted. "Return it to me at once!"

"Whoops! How did *that* end up in my pocket?" Mr. Green said with fake innocence. Tears were streaming down his face. "I can't find my hankie. Does someone have one I might borrow?"

Mrs. Peacock opened her purse. "I hope you don't include me in your den of thieves," she told Mr. Boddy. "It's bad manners to insult your guests without proof."

Mrs. Peacock located her lace handkerchief and drew it from her purse. To her horror, one of Mr. Boddy's antique gold spoons tumbled from it.

"Let me guess — my spoon," Mr. Boddy said with a sigh. "Mrs. Peacock, now what do you have to say for yourself?"

"I say I had every intention of returning the spoon," she replied, "once I had it cleaned and polished for you, my dear friend."

Mr. Boddy stared at his guests. "You are impossible!"

"Surely you don't include me in their company," said Professor Plum, pointing to Colonel Mustard, Mr. Green, and Mrs. Peacock.

"Yes, Plum and I are your true friends," insisted Miss Scarlet.

But Mr. Boddy had heard enough.

"All right now, empty your pockets," he ordered. "Return what you were hoping to steal."

"And if we refuse?" asked a stubborn Miss Scarlet.

"Then you'll leave me no other choice but to turn you over to the police," said Mr. Boddy.

"In that case, I'll go first," said Professor Plum. "Mr. Boddy, first let me say how ashamed I feel. You've been a wonderful friend all these years. Please forgive me." Crying like a baby, Professor Plum turned over Mr. Boddy's heirloom silver cup.

"I'm sorry, too," said Miss Scarlet. She returned Mr. Boddy's mother's ruby tiara.

"As long as everyone else is coming clean, so should I," added Mrs. White. She gave Mr. Boddy back the gold pocket watch she'd pickpocketed earlier that evening.

"I'm very disappointed," Mr. Boddy said, shaking his head. "And to think that this very night I was planning to fill out my life insurance policy and name my beneficiary."

"Beneficiary?" echoed Miss Scarlet. "You mean the person who will receive a small token sum of money upon your untimely death?"

"Precisely," Mr. Boddy said. "A small token sum in the order of *three million dollars!*"

Mr. Boddy showed his guests the policy he had recently purchased. "Not only did I receive this policy," he said, "I received a lovely certificate suitable for framing, too!"

He showed them the blank line where he had yet to write in the name of his beneficiary.

"I think there's just enough room to put in my name," suggested Mr. Green. "Try it. Go ahead and write capital G, r-e — "

" — e-d!" finished Miss Scarlet. "Greed, not Green, should be his name." She took a fountain pen from her purse. "This contains beautiful red ink. The perfect color with which to write in *my* name."

"Blue would be a better choice," said Mrs. Peacock, thrusting her own fountain pen in Boddy's direction.

"Don't listen to them," said Colonel Mustard. He elbowed his way to the front. "I'm your real friend. We go together like a hot dog and mustard."

"Don't insult your host by calling him a hot dog," said Mrs. White. "He's a filet mignon! After all of my years of loyal service, I should get to be the beneficiary."

"No, me!" insisted Professor Plum.

"Why you, Professor?" asked Mr. Boddy.

"Give me a few minutes to think and I'll come up with a reason," begged Professor Plum.

"Let's see how our last night together in the mansion goes," Mr. Boddy insisted. "I'm keeping an extra close eye on all of you. By morning I should know who most deserves to be named my beneficiary."

With that, Mr. Boddy returned the policy to the inside pocket of his jacket.

Several hours later . . .

Several hours later, Mr. Boddy left the Library and finished some last-minute business in the Study.

On his way out, he turned out the light.

He moved to the Hall, where he made certain

that the front door was locked. There he lit the candle in the Candlestick, and turned off the electric chandelier.

With the only light coming from the candle, Mr. Boddy stopped at the foot of the stairs. He listened, and to his surprise, he heard no unusual noises coming from the guest bedrooms above.

"Hmmm," Mr. Boddy said to himself. "Maybe I misjudged my guests. Maybe they *are* the best friends a person could ever — "

Just then, someone jumped from the shadows and strangled Mr. Boddy with the Rope.

The murderer searched Mr. Boddy's clothes to find the insurance policy. The murderer took it and the Candlestick, and left the Rope twisted around Mr. Boddy's neck.

Hearing someone approaching, the murderer fled into the Billiard Room, where a male guest was about to shoot a game of pool.

"You're up very late," said the murderer, suddenly very composed.

"This news about the insurance policy kept me awake," the male guest replied. "I thought a game of billiards might calm me down."

The murderer placed the Candlestick on the edge of the billiard table. "I thought you might enjoy a bit more light," the murderer said. "If you don't mind my company, I'd enjoy a quick game of — "

But before she could finish her sentence, Mr.

Boddy's murderer was attacked by the male guest with the Wrench.

Mr. Boddy's murderer collapsed to the floor.

"Serves you right, you old bird!" crowed the male guest.

He took the insurance policy and fled into the Dining Room, where he encountered Mrs. White polishing the silver.

"Mrs. White, what are you doing up at this late hour?" he asked.

"Working, as usual," she said.

"In that case, would you be so kind as to fetch me a late-night snack?" he said.

"Come with me," she said, leaving the Dining Room. "If you're forcing me to open the pantry, at least give me the pleasure of your company."

The two went into the Kitchen, where — to the male guest's surprise — Mrs. White squirted him in the eyes with a bottle of bright yellow condiment, which temporarily blinded him.

"Now *you're* the hot dog! I had an idea you were up to no good," she said over his felled body. She reached down and retrieved the insurance policy. Then she escaped through the secret passage and emerged in the Study.

But Professor Plum was waiting and knocked her out with the Lead Pipe. "I saw you going into the Dining Room and knew you were plotting something. And, as you can see," he said, "the secret passage isn't very secret."

He took the insurance policy from Mrs. White's apron and fled to the Conservatory.

There, he put down the Lead Pipe and was about to pen his name in as Mr. Boddy's beneficiary — when he was shot.

Professor Plum's attacker picked up the insurance policy and dashed into the Lounge, where he hid the weapon and silencer used to shoot the professor.

A moment later, he was about to write his own name on the policy when he was attacked by a female guest with the only weapon not used so far this evening.

She, in turn, took the insurance policy into the only room not visited yet this evening, where she boldly penned in her name as Mr. Boddy's beneficiary.

WHO KILLED MR. BODDY?
WHO USED WHAT WEAPON AND ENDED
UP IN WHICH ROOM WITH THE
INSURANCE POLICY?

SOLUTION

MRS. PEACOCK with the ROPE.
MISS SCARLET used the KNIFE, then went
to the BALL ROOM.

We know that Mr. Boddy's murderer is a woman. It can't be Mrs. White because she was in the Dining Room.

We also know that a female guest ended up with the insurance policy. Can it be the same person? The answer is no. In the Billiard Room, Mr. Boddy's murderer was referred to as "you old bird." This makes sense only in reference to Mrs. Peacock. Her attacker was a male guest who was later blinded by his namesake yellow condiment, mustard.

Professor Plum is identified by name. This leaves Mr. Green as Professor Plum's attacker. Since Mrs. White, Mrs. Peacock, and Colonel Mustard have been eliminated, Miss Scarlet must be the last guest to end up with the policy.

All rooms but the Ball Room are named, and all weapons but the Knife are named or referred to.